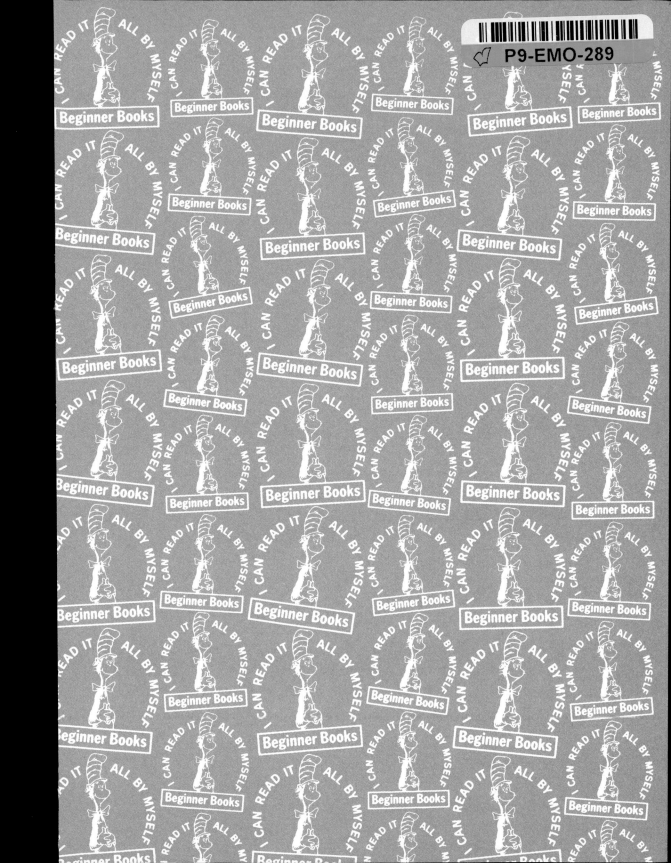

Copyright © 2005 by Peter Anthony Eastman.
All rights reserved under International and Pan-American Copyright Conventions. Published in the United States by Random House Children's Books, a division of Random House, Inc., New York, and simultaneously in Canada by Random House of Canada Limited, Toronto.
Featuring the characters Fred and Ted, copyright © 1973 by P. D. Eastman. Copyright renewed 2001 by Mary L. Eastman, Peter Anthony Eastman, and Alan Eastman.

www.randomhouse.com/kids

Library of Congress Cataloging-in-Publication Data
Eastman, Peter, 1942–
Fred and Ted go camping / by Peter Eastman. — 1st ed.
    p.   cm. — "Beginner books."
SUMMARY: Even though they do things very differently, friends Fred and Ted enjoy going camping together in the woods.
ISBN 0-375-82965-2 (trade) — ISBN 0-375-92965-7 (lib. bdg.)
[1. Camping—Fiction. 2. Individuality—Fiction. 3. Dogs—Fiction.]
I. Title. II. Series.   PZ7.E13153Fr 2005   [E]—dc22   2004007481

Printed in the United States of America   First Edition   20

Fred and Ted Go Camping

by Peter Eastman

BEGINNER BOOKS®

A Division of Random House, Inc.

Fred and Ted were friends.

They liked to go camping in the woods.

One day they packed their cars.

They were going camping.

They drove to the woods.

Fred took many things.

Ted took few things.

They parked their cars
and walked into the woods.

Fred liked this spot.

Ted liked it, too.

Fred had a hard time with his tent.

Ted had an easy time with his tent.

That night,

Fred was awake.

Ted was asleep.

The next morning . . .

Ted woke up early.

Fred woke up late.

They took their boat to the lake.

Fred took the heavy end.

Ted took the light end.

They put the boat in the water.
Ted stayed dry.

Fred got wet.

They fished.

Ted used a net.

Fred used a pole.

Ted got ten little fish.

Fred got one BIG fish!

Splash!

The boat tipped over!

All the little fish
jumped out.

Fred and Ted swam away
from the big fish!

Ted swam fast.

Fred swam faster.

Then they heard a little bird.

"Look up in a tree.

Look down at your feet.

And you will soon find

something to eat,"

sang the little bird.

Fred looked up.

He saw nothing.

Ted looked down.

He saw something.

Berries!

Fred looked up again.

Bonk!

Something hit Fred on his head.

They even found some crab apples.

They went back to camp.

Ted ran with the berries.

Fred walked with the
apples and nuts.

They cooked the apples
and the nuts
in a pan
on a fire.

They ate it all up.

Ted ate slowly.

Fred ate quickly.

What about the berries?

They saved the berries for last.

Yum!

Peter Eastman is the son of P. D. Eastman (1909–1986), author/illustrator of *Are You My Mother?, Go, Dog. Go!, The Best Nest,* and many other beloved children's books.

Peter followed his father into the animation field, working as an award-winning animator/director. *Fred and Ted Go Camping* is his first book.